Front-Page News

adapted by Jodie Shepherd
adapted from the screenplay "Front Page News" by Scott Gray
illustrated by Carlo Lo Raso

Ready-to-Read

SIMON SPOTLIGHT/NICKELODEON
New York   London   Toronto   Sydney

Based on the TV series *Nick Jr. The Backyardigans*™ as seen on Nick Jr.®

SIMON SPOTLIGHT
An imprint of Simon & Schuster Children's Publishing Division
1230 Avenue of the Americas, New York, New York 10020
© 2010 Viacom International Inc. All rights reserved.
NICK JR., *Nick Jr. The Backyardigans*, and all related titles, logos, and characters are trademarks
of Viacom International Inc. NELVANA™ Nelvana Limited. CORUS™ Corus Entertainment Inc.
For information about special discounts for bulk purchases, please contact
Simon & Schuster Special Sales at 1-866-506-1949 or business@simonandschuster.com.
Manufactured in the United States of America, 0110 LAK
First Edition
2 4 6 8 10 9 7 5 3 1
Library of Congress Cataloging-in-Publication Data
Shepherd, Jodie.
Front page news / adapted by Jodie Shepherd ; adapted from the episode "Front Page News"
by Scott Gray ; illustrated by Carlo Lo Raso. — 1st ed.
p. cm. — (Ready-to-read)
"Based on the TV series Nick Jr. The Backyardigans as seen on Nick Jr."—Copyright p.
ISBN 978-1-4169-8569-3
I. Gray, Scott. II. Lo Raso, Carlo. III. Backyardigans (Television program) IV. Title.
PZ7.S54373Fr 2010
[E]—dc22
2009023720

'Snap! I am .
TASHA

I take for a ."
PICTURES   NEWSPAPER

 has another job, too.
TASHA

'But shhh! It is a secret.

Nobody knows but you!"

"I am Super Snap,

a superspeedy superhero."

 says.

TASHA

"I zip, zoom, spin, and snap.

I rescue those in need."

's boss is .

TASHA   PABLO

He runs the .

NEWSPAPER

The is called

NEWSPAPER

Bigopolis Big News.

"Say ' !'" says to .

CHEESE TASHA PABLO

"We have a problem, kid,"

answers .

PABLO

"There is no news and no

PICTURE

for the front page!"

'I will get a for you,"

PICTURE

 says.

TASHA

'It has always been my dream

to take a front-page ."

PICTURE

The rings.
TELEPHONE

"A giant is on Big Sea !"
ROBOT   BRIDGE

exclaims .
PABLO

" is going to stop him?"
CAPTAIN BUBBLE

'Do not worry, boss," says .

TASHA

'I am on my way.

I will find and

CAPTAIN BUBBLE

the .

ROBOT

I will take a in a snap!"

PICTURE

"Wherever there is trouble,

I am there on the !"
BUBBLE

says .
CAPTAIN BUBBLE

He points his .
WAND

He traps the inside a big
ROBOT   BUBBL

'Say ' !'" says .
CHEESE   TASHA

The is running away.
BUBBLE

The is on the loose!
ROBOT

"Oh, no!" cries .
TASHA

" needs help!"
CAPTAIN BUBBLE

It is a job for Super Snap!"

 snaps. spins.
TASHA   TASHA

 makes a !
TASHA   TORNADO

The carries the away.
TORNADO   ROBOT

There is no ▨ for the ▨ .
PICTURE   NEWSPAPER

 will not be happy," says .
PABLO   TASHA

is **not** happy.

PABLO

"Now we have no news.

The rings.

TELEPHONE

"Hello?" answers .

PABLO

'The is at the airport?
ROBOT

 will save the day?"
BUG GIRL

'And I will snap a ," says .
PICTURE   TASHA

The   is on the runway.

ROBOT

 tries to lift the

BUG GIRL   ROBOT

off of the runway.

Whoa! It is hard work.

needs help fast.

BUG GIRL

Super Snap to the rescue!

The takes off into the .

ROBOT   CLOUDS

Still there is no .
PICTURE

 is **really** not happy.
PABLO

"We will never get a now!"
PICTURE

The rings.
TELEPHONE

Look behind me?" asks .
PABLO

Through the he sees the !
WINDOW   ROBOT

And !
CAPTAIN BUBBLE

nd !
BUG GIRL

buzzes around the

BUG GIRL   ROBOT

while makes

CAPTAIN BUBBLE

a wall.

BUBBLE

They stop the !

ROBOT

"Say ' !'" says .
CHEESE TASHA

Crash! The is so excited,
ROBOT

he breaks the ● wall.
BUBBLE

 are everywhere!
BUBBLES

" , , ," cries the

CHEESE   CHEESE   CHEESE   ROBOT

 says, "The doesn't

TASHA   ROBOT

want to **eat** .

CHEESE

The wants to **say** ' '."

ROBOT   CHEESE

So uses her timer. **Snap!**

TASHA

'Great !" says .

PICTURE   PABLO

'You saved my !

NEWSPAPER

'You saved the town, too!"

There is one more thing to do.

It is superhero snack time.

" !" everyone shouts.

CHEESE

WITHDRAWN